The Informal Execution

of

Soupbone Pew

and other short stories

by

Damon Runyon

Contents

The Informal Execution of Soupbone Pew

What is it the Good Book says? I read it last night--it said:
That he who sheddeth another man's blood by man shall his
blood be shed!
That's as fair as a man could ask it, who lives by the gun and
knife--
But the Law don't give him an even break when it's taking away
his life.

Ho, the Law's unfair when it uses a chair, and a jolt from an un-
seen Death;
Or it makes him flop to a six--foot drop and a rope shuts off his
breath;
If he's got to die let him die by the Book, with a Death that he
can see.
By a gun or knife, as he went through life, and both legs kicking
free!
> *--Songs of the "Shut-Ins"*

THE condemned man in the cell next to us laughed in-
cessantly. He had been sentenced that morning, and they told us
he had started laughing as soon as the words, "May the Lord
have mercy on your soul," were pronounced. He was to be taken
to the penitentiary next day to await execution.

Chicago Red had manifested a lively interest in the case. The man had killed a railroad brakeman, so one of the guards told us; had killed him coldly, and without provocation. The trial had commenced since our arrival at the county jail and had lasted three days, during which time Red talked of little else.

From the barred windows of the jail corridor, when we were exercising, we could see the dingy old criminal court across the yard and Red watched the grim procession to and from the jail each day. He speculated on the progress of the trial; he knew when the case went to the jury, and when he saw the twelve men, headed by the two old bailiffs returning after lunch the third day, he announced:

"They've got the verdict, and it's first degree murder. They ain't talking and not a one has even grinned."

Then when the unfortunate was brought back, laughing that dismal laugh, Red said:

"He's nutty. He was nutty to go. It ain't exactly right to swing that guy."

Red and I were held as suspects in connection with an affair which had been committed a full forty--eight hours before we landed in town. We had no particular fear of being implicated in the matter, and the officers had no idea that we had anything to do with it, but they were holding us as evidence to the public that they were working on the case. We had been "vagged" for ten days each.

It was no new experience for us in any respect--not even the condemned man, for we had frequently been under the same roof with men sentenced to die. The only unusual feature was Red's interest in the laughing man.

"Red," I asked, as we sat playing cards, "did you ever kill a man?"

He dropped a card calmly, taking the trick, and as he contemplated his hand, considering his next lead, he answered:

"For why do you ask me that?"

"Oh, I don't know; I just wondered," I said. "You've seen and done so many things that I thought you might accidentally have met with something of the sort." "It isn't exactly a polite question," he replied. "I've seen some murders. I've seen quite a few, in fact. I've seen some pulled off in a chief's private office, when they was sweating some poor still; and I've seen some, other places."

"Did you ever kill a man?" I insisted.

He studied my lead carefully.

"I never did," he finally answered. "That is to say, I never bumped no guy off personal. I never had nothing to do with no job from which come ghosts to wake me up at night and bawl me out."

"They say a guy what kills a man never closes his eyes again, even when he really sleeps. I go to the hay, and my eyes are shut tight, so I know I ain't to be held now or hereafter for nothing like that."

We finished the game in silence, and Red seemed very thoughtful. He laid the cards aside, rolled a cigarette, and said; "Listen! I never killed no guy personal, like I say; I mean for nothing he done to me. I've been a gun and crook for many years, like you know, but I'm always mighty careful about hurting anyone permanent. I'm careful about them pete jobs, so's not to blow up no harmless persons, and I always tell my outside men that, when they have to do shooting, not to try to hit anyone. If they did, accidental, that ain't my fault. One reason I took to inside work was to keep from having to kill anyone. I've been so close to being taken that I could hear the gates of the Big House slam, and one little shot would have saved me a lot of trouble, but I always did my best to keep from letting that shot go. I never wanted to kill no man. I've been in jams where guys were after me good and strong, and I always tried to get by without no killings.

3

"I said I never killed a guy. I helped once, but it wasn't murder. It's never worried me a bit since, and I sleep good."

He walked to the window and peered out into the yard where a bunch of sparrows were fluttering about. Finally he turned and said:

"I hadn't thought of that for quite a while, and I never do until I see some poor stiff that's been tagged to go away. Some of them make me nervous--especially this tee--hee guy next to us. I'll tell you about Soupbone Pew--some day you can write it, if you want to."

Soupbone Pew was a rat who trained years ago with Billy Coulon, the Honey Grove Kid, and a bunch of other old--timers that you've never seen. It was before my time, too, but I've heard them talk about him. He was in the Sioux City bank tear--off, when they all got grabbed and were sent to the Big House for fifteen years each. In them days Soupbone was a pretty good guy. He had nerve, and was smart, and stood well with everybody, but a little stretch in the big stir got to him.

He broke bad. Honey Grove laid a plan for a big spring--a get--away-- while they were up yonder. It looked like it would go through, too, but just as they were about ready, Soupbone got cold feet and gave up his insides.

For that he got a pardon, and quit the road right off. He became a railroad brakeman, and showed up as a shack running between Dodge City and La Junta. And he became the orneriest white man that God ever let live, too.

To hoboes and guns he was like a reformed soak toward a drunk He treated them something fierce. He was a big, powerful stiff, who could kill a man with a wallop of his hands, if he hit him right, and his temper soured on the world. Most likely it was because he was afraid that every guy on the road was out to get him because of what he'd done, or maybe it was because he knew that they knew he was yellow. Anyway, they never tried to do him, that job belonging to Coulon, Honey Grove and the others..Soupbone cracked that no 'bo could ride his division, and he made it good, too. He beat them up when they tried it, and he made it so strong that the old heads wouldn't go against a try when he was the run. Once in a while some kid took a stab at it, but if he got caught by Soupbone he regretted it the rest of his life. I've heard of that little road into Hot Springs, where they say a reward used to be offered to any 'bo that rode it, and how a guy beat it by getting in the water--tank; and I've personally met that Wyoming gent on the Union Pacific, and all them other guys they say is so tough, but them stories is only fairy--tales for children beside what could be told about Pew. He went an awful route.

I've known of him catching guys in the pilot and throwing scalding water in on them; I've heard tell of him shoveling hot cinders into empties on poor bums laying there asleep. That trick of dropping a coupling--pin on the end of a wire down alongside a moving train, so that it would swing up underneath and knock a stiff off the rods, was about the mildest thing he did.

He was simply a devil. The other railroad men on the division wouldn't hardly speak to him.

They couldn't stand his gaff, but they couldn't very well roar at him keeping 'boes off his trains because that was what he was there for.

His longest suit was beating guys up. He just loved to catch some poor old broken--down bum on his train and pound the everlasting stuffing out of him. He's sent many a guy to the hospital, and maybe he killed a few before my acquaintance with him, for all I know.

Once in a while he ran against some live one--some real gun, and not a bum--who'd given him a battle, but he was there forty ways with a sap and gat, and he'd shoot as quick as he'd slug.

He didn't go so strong on the real guns, if he knew who they was, and I guess he was always afraid they might be friends of Honey Grove or Coulon.

He was on the run when I first heard of him, and some of the kids of my day would try to pot him from the road, when his train went by, but they never even come close. I've heard them talking of pulling a rail on him and letting his train go into the ditch, but that would have killed the other trainmen, and they was some good guys on that same run then. The best way to do was to fight shy of Soupbone, and keep him on ice for Honey Grove and Coulon.

Training with our mob in them days was a young kid called Manchester Slim--a real kid, not over eighteen, and as nice and quiet a youngster as I ever see. He wasn't cut out for the road. It seems he'd had some trouble at home and run away. Old man Muller, that Dutch prowler, used to have him on his staff, but he never let this kid in on any work for some reason. He was always trying to get Slim to go home.

"Der road is hell for der kits," he used to say. "Let der ole stiffs vork out dere string, und don't make no new vuns."

The Slim paid no attention to him. Still he had no great love for the life, and probably would have quit long before if he hadn't been afraid some one would think he was scared off.

They was a pete job on at La Junta, which me and 'Frisco Shine and Muller had laid out. We had jungled up--camped--in a little cottonwood grove a few miles out of town, and was boiling out soup--nitro-- glycerine--from dynamite, you know--and Muller sent the Slim into town to look around a bit. It was winter and pretty cold. We had all come in from the West and was headed East. We was all broke bad, too, and needed dough the worst way.

Slim come back from town much excited. He was carrying a Denver newspaper in his hand.

"I've got to go home, Mull," he said, running up to the old man and holding out the paper.

"Look at this ad."

Muller read it and called to me. He showed me a little want ad reading that Gordon Keleher, who disappeared from his home in Boston two years before, was wanted at home because his mother was dying. It was signed Pelias Keleher, and I knew who he was, all right--president of the National Bankers' Association.

"Well, you go," I said, right off the reel, and I could see that was the word he was waiting for.

"For certainly he goes," said Muller. "Nail der next rattler."

"All the passengers are late, but there's a freight due out of here tonight; I asked," said Slim.

"How much dough iss dere in dis mob?" demanded Muller, frisking himself. We all shook ourselves down, but the most we could scare up was three or four dollars.

"If you could wait until after tonight," I says, thinking of the job, but Muller broke me off with:

"Ve don't vant him to vait. Somedings might happens."

"I'd wire home for money, but I want to get to Kansas City first," said Slim. "That paper is a couple of days old, and there's no telling how long it may have been running that ad. I can stop over in K.C. long enough to get plenty of dough from some people I know there. I'm going to grab that freight."

"Soupbone on dat freight," said the 'Frisco Shine, a silent, wicked black.

"Ve'll see Soub," said Muller quietly. "I guess maybe he von't inderfere mit dis case."

We decided to abandon the job for the night, and all went uptown. The Slim was apparently very much worried, and he kept telling us that if he didn't get home in time he'd never forgive himself, so we all got dead--set on seeing him started.

We looked up the conductor of the freight due out that night and explained things to him. None of us knew him, but he was a nice fellow.

"I tell you, boys," he said, "I'd let the young fellow ride, but you'd better see my head brakeman, Soupbone Pew. He's a tough customer, but in a case like this he ought to be all right."

"I'll speak to him myself."

Muller went after Pew. He found him in a saloon, drinking all by his lonesome, although there was a crowd of other railroad men in there at the time. Muller knew Pew in the old days, but there was no sign of recognition between them. The old Dutchman explained to Pew very briefly.

"It vould pe a greed personal favor mit me, Soub; maype somedimes I return it."

"He can't ride my train!" said Pew shortly. "That's flat. No argument goes."

The Dutchman looked at him long and earnestly, murder showing in his eyes, and Pew slunk back close to the bar, and his hand dropped to his hip.

"Soub, der poy rides!" said Muller, his voice low but shaking with anger. "He rides your rattler. Und if anyding happens by dot poy, de Honey Grove Kit von't get no chance at you! Dot's all, Soub!"

But when he returned to us, he was plainly afraid for the Slim.

"You don't bedder go to--nid," he said. "Dot Soub is a defil, und he'll do you."

"I'm not afraid," said Slim. "He can't find me, anyhow."

The old man tried to talk him out of the idea, but Slim was determined, and finally Muller, in admiration of his spirit, said:

"Vell, if you vill go, you vill. Vun man can hide besser as two, but der Shine must go mit you as far as Dodge."

That was the only arrangement he would consent to, and while the Slim didn't want the Shine, and I myself couldn't see what good he could do, Muller insisted so strong that we all gave in..We went down to the yards that night to see them off, and the old man had a private confab with the Shine. The only time I ever saw Muller show any feeling was when he told the boy goodby. I guess he really liked him.

The two hid back of a pile of ties, a place where the trains slowed down, and me and Muller got off a distance and watched them. We could see Soupbone standing on top of a box--car as the train went by, and he looked like a tall devil. He was trying to watch both sides of the train at the same time, but I didn't think he saw either Slim or the Shine as they shot under-neath the cars, one after the other, and nailed the rods. Then the tram went off into the darkness, Soupbone standing up straight and stiff.

We went back to our camp to sleep, and the next morn-ing before we were awake, the Shine came limping in, covered with blood and one arm hanging at his side.

I didn't have to hear his story to guess what had hap-pened. Soupbone made them at the first stop. He hadn't expected two, but he did look for the kid. Instead of warning him off, he told him to get on top where he'd be safe. That was one of his old tricks. He didn't get to the Shine, who dodged off into the darkness, as soon as he found they were grabbed, and then caught the train after it started again. He crawled up between the cars to the deck, to tip the Slim off to watch out for Soupbone. Slim didn't suspect anything, and was thanking Soupbone, and explaining about his mother.

The moment the train got under way good, Soupbone says:

"Now my pretty boy, you're such a--good traveler, let's see you jump off this train!"

The kid thought he was joshing, but there wasn't no josh about it. Soup pulled a gun. The Shine, with his own gun in hand, crawled clear on top and lay flat on the cars, trying to steady his aim on Soupbone. The kid was pleading and almost crying, when Soupbone suddenly jumped at him, smashed him in the jaw with the gun--barrel, and knocked him off the train. The Shine shot Soupbone in the back, and he dropped on top of the train, but didn't roll off. As the Shine was going down between the cars again, Souphone shot at him and broke his arm. He got off all right, and went back down the road to find the kid dead--his neck broke.

Old man Muller, the mildest man in the world generally, almost went bug--house when he heard that spiel. He raved and tore around like a sure enough nut. I've known him to go backing out of a town with every man in his mob down on the ground, dead or dying, and not show half as much feeling afterward. You'd 'a' thought the kid was his own. He swore he'd do nothing else as long as he lived until he'd cut Soupbone's heart out.

The Shine had to get out of sight, because Soupbone would undoubtedly have some wild--eyed story to tell about being attacked by hoboes and being shot by one. We had no hope but what the Shine had killed him.

Old man Muller went into town and found out that was just what had happened, and he was in the hospital only hurt a little. He also found they'd brought Slim's body to town, and that most people suspected the real truth, too. He told them just how it was, especially the railroad men, and said the Shine had got out of the country. He also wired Slim's people, and we heard afterward they sent a special train after the remains.

Muller was told, too, that the train conductor had notified Pew to let Slim ride, and that the rest of the train--crew had served notice on Pew that if he threw the boy off he'd settle with them for it. And that was just what made Soupbone anxious to get the kid. It ended his railroad career there, as we found out afterwards, because he disappeared as soon as he got out of the hospital.

Meantime me and Muller and the Shine went ahead with that job, and it failed. Muller and the nigger got grabbed, and I had a tough time getting away. Just before we broke camp the night before, however, Muller, who seemed to have a hunch that something was going to happen, called me and the Shine to him, and said, his voice solemn:

"I vant you poys to bromise me vun ting," he said. "If I don't get der chance myself, bromise me dot venefer you find Soubbone Bew, you vill kill him deat."

And we promised, because we didn't think we would ever be called on to make good.

Muller got a long jolt for the job; the Shine got a shorter one and escaped a little bit later on, while I left that part of the country.

A couple of years later, on a bitter cold night, in a certain town that I won't name, there was five of us in the sneezer, held as suspects on a house prowl job that only one of us had anything to do with--I ain't mentioning the name of the one, either. They was me, Kid Mole, the old prize--fighter, a hophead named Squirt McCue, that you don't know, Jew Friend, a dip, and that same 'Frisco Shine. We were all in the bull--pen with a mixed assortment of drunks and vags. All kinds of prisoners was put in there over night. This pokey is down-- stairs under the police station, not a million miles from the Missouri River, so if you think hard you can guess the place. We were walking around kidding the drunks, when a screw shoved in a long, tall guy who acted like he was drunk or nutty, and was hardly able to stand.

I took one flash at his map, and I knew him. It was Pew.

He flopped down in a corner as soon as the screw let go his arm. The Shine rapped to him as quick as I did, and officed Mole and the rest. They all knew of him, especially the Honey Grove business, as well as about the Manchester Slim, for word had gone over the country at the time.

11

As soon as the screw went up--stairs I walked over to the big stiff, laying all huddled up, and poked him with my foot.

"What's the matter with you, you big cheese?" I said. He only mumbled.

"Stand up!" I tells him, but he didn't stir. The Shine and Mole got hold of him on either side and lifted him to his feet. He was as limber as a wet bar--towel. Just then we heard the screw coming down-- stairs and we got away from Pew. The screw brought in a jag--a laughing jag--a guy with his snoot full of booze and who laughed like he'd just found a lot of money. He was a little, thin fellow, two pounds lighter than a straw hat. He laughed high and shrill, more like a scream than a real laugh, and the moment the screw opened the door and tossed him in, something struck me that the laugh was phoney. It didn't sound on the level.

There wasn't no glad in it. The little guy laid on the floor and kicked his feet and kept on laughing. Soupbone Pew let out a yell at the sight of him.

"Don't let him touch me!" he bawled, rolling over against the wall. "Don't let him near me!"

"Why, you big stiff, you could eat him alive!" I says.

The jag kept on tee--heeing, not looking at us, or at Pew either for that matter.

"He's nuts," said Jew Friend.

"Shut him off," I told the Shine.

He stepped over and picked the jag up with one hand, held him out at arm's length, and walloped him on the jaw with his other hand. The jag went to sleep with a laugh sticking in his throat. Soupbone still lay against the wall moaning, but he saw that business all right, and it seemed to help him. The Shine tossed the jag into a cell. Right after that the screw came down with another drunk, and I asked him about Pew.

"Who's this boob?" I said. "Is he sick?"

"Him? Oh, he's a good one," said screw. "He only killed his poor wife--beat her to death with his two fists, because she didn't have supper ready on time, or something important. That ain't his blood on him; that's hers. He's pretty weak, now, hey? Well, he wasn't so weak a couple of hours ago, the rat! It's the wickedest murder ever done in this town, and he'll hang sure, if he ain't lynched beforehand!"

He gave Soupbone a kick as he went out, and Soupbone groaned.

Said I: "It's got to be done, gents; swing or no swing, this guy has got to go. Who is it--me?"

"Me!" said the Shine, stepping forward.

"Me!" said the Jew.

"Me!" chimed in Mole.

"All of us!" said the hophead.

"Stand him up!" I ordered.

The lights had been turned down low, and it was dark and shadowy in the jail. The only sound was the soft pad--pad of people passing through the snow on the sidewalks above our heads, the low sizzling of the water--spout at the sink, and the snores of the drunks, who were all asleep.

Us five was the only ones awake. The Shine and Mole lifted Soupbone up, and this time he was not so limp. He seemed to know that something was doing. His eyes was wide open and staring at us.

"Pew," I said in a whisper, "do you remember the kid you threw off your rattler three years ago?"

"And shot me in the arm?" asked Shine.

Pew couldn't turn any whiter, but his eyes rolled back into his head.

"Don't!" he whispered. "Don't say that. It made me crazy! I'm crazy now! I was crazy when I killed that little girl tonight. It

13

was all on account of thinking about him. He comes to see me often."

"Well, Pew," I said, "a long time back you were elected to die. I was there when the sentence was passed, and it'd been carried out a long time ago if you hadn't got away. I guess we'll have to kill you tonight."

"Don't, boys!" he whined. "I ain't fit to die! Don't hurt me!"

"Why, you'll swing anyway!" said Friend.

"No! My God, no!" he said. "I was crazy; I'm crazy now, and they don't hang crazy people!"

I was standing square in front of him. His head had raised a little as he talked and his jaw was sticking out. I suddenly made a move with my left hand, as though to slap him, and he showed that his mind was active enough by dodging, so that it brought his jaw out further, and he said, "Don't." Then I pulled my right clear from my knee and took him on the point of the jaw. The Shine and Mole jumped back. Soupbone didn't fall; he just slid down in a heap, like his body had melted into his shoes.

We all jumped for him at the same time, but an idea popped into my head, and I stopped them.

Soupbone was knocked out, but he was coming back fast. You can't kill a guy like that by hitting him. The jail was lighted by a few incandescent lights, and one of them was hung on a wire that reached down from the ceiling over the sink, and had a couple of feet of it coiled up in the middle. Uncoiled, the light would reach clear to the floor. I pointed to it, but the bunch didn't get my idea right away. The switch for the lights was inside the bull--pen, and I turned them off. I had to work fast for fear the screw upstairs would notice the lights was out and come down to see what the trouble was. A big arc outside threw a little glim through the sidewalk grating, so I could see what I was doing.

I uncoiled the wire and sawed it against the edge of the sink, close to the lamp, until it came in two. Then I bared the wire back for a foot. The gang tumbled, and carried Pew over to where the wire would reach him. I unfastened his collar, looped the naked end of the wire around his neck and secured it. By this time he was about come to, but he didn't seem to realize what was going on.

All but me got into their cells and I stepped over and turned the switch--button just as Pew was struggling to his feet. The voltage hit him when he was on all fours. He stood straight up, stiff, like a soldier at salute. There was a strange look on his face--a surprised look. Then, as though someone had hit him from behind, his feet left the floor and he swung straight out to the length of the wire and it broke against his weight, just as I snapped off the current. Pew dropped to the floor and curled up like a big singed spider, and a smell like frying bacon filled the room.

I went over and felt of his heart. It was still beating, but very light.

"They ain't enough current," whispered Mole. "We got to do it some other way."

"Hang him wid de wire," said the Shine.

"Aw--nix!" spoke up the Jew. "I tell you that makes me sick--bumping a guy off that way. Hanging and electricity, see? That's combining them too much. Let's use the boot."

"It ain't fair, kind--and that's a fact," whispered McCue. "It's a little too legal. The boot! Give him the boot!"

The voice of the screw came singing down the stairs:

"Is that big guy awake?"

"Yes," I shouted back, "we're all awake; he won't let us sleep."

"Tell him he'd better say his prayers!" yelled the screw. "I just got word a mob is forming to come and get him!"

"Let him alone," I whispered to the gang. Mole was making a noose of the wire, and the Shine had hunted up a bucket to stand Pew on. They drew back and Soupbone lay stretched out on the floor.

I went over and felt of his heart again. I don't remember whether I felt any beat or not. I couldn't have said I did, at the moment, and I couldn't say I didn't. I didn't have time to make sure, because suddenly there run across the floor something that looked to me like a shadow, or a big rat. Then the shrill laugh of that jag rattled through the bull--pen. He slid along half--stooped, as quick as a streak of light, and before we knew what was doing he had pounced on Soupbone and had fastened his hands tight around the neck of the big stiff. He was laughing that crazy laugh all the time.

"I'll finish him for you!" he squeaked. He fastened his hands around Soupbone's neck. I kicked the jag in the side of the head as hard as I could, but it didn't faze him. The bunch laid hold of him and pulled, but they only dragged Soupbone all over the place. Finally the jag let go and stood up, and we could see he wasn't no more drunk than we was. He let loose that laugh once more, and just as the Shine started the bucket swinging for his head, he said: "I'm her brother!" Then he went down kicking.

We went into our cells and crawled into our bunks. Soupbone lay outside. The Shine pulled the jag into a corner. I tell you true, I went to sleep right away. I thought the screw would find out when he brought the next drunk down, but it woke up by a big noise on the stairs. The door flew open with a bang, and a gang of guys came down, wild--eyed and yelling. The screw was with them and they had tight hold of him.

"Keep in, you men!" he bawled to us..."That's your meat!" he said to the gang, pointing at what had been Soupbone. The men pounced on him like a lot of hounds on to a rabbit, and before you could bat an eye they had a rope around Soupbone's neck and was tearing up the stairs again, dragging him along.

They must have thought he was asleep; they never noticed that he didn't move a muscle himself, and they took the person of Soupbone Pew, or anyways what had been him, outside and hung it over a telegraph wire.

We saw it there when we was sprung next morning. When the screw noticed the blood around the bull--pen, he said:

"Holy smoke, they handled him rough!" And he never knew no different.

If the mob hadn't come--but the mob did come, and so did the laughing jag. I left him that morning watching the remains of Soupbone Pew.

"She was my sister," he said to me.

I don't know for certain whether we killed Soupbone, whether the jag did it, or whether the mob finished him; but he was dead, and he ought to have died. Sometimes I wonder a bit about it, but no ghosts come to me, like I say, so I can't tell.

They's an unmarked grave in the potter's field of this town I speak of, and once in a while I go there when I'm passing through and meditate on the sins of Soupbone Pew. But I sleep well of nights. I done what had to be done, and I close my eyes and I don't never see Soupbone Pew.

He turned once more to gazing out of the window.

"Well, what is there about condemned men to make you so nervous?" I demanded.

"I said some condemned men," he replied, still gazing. "Like this guy next door."

A loud, shrill laugh rang through the corridors.

"He's that same laughing jag," said Chicago Red.

The End

17

Dancing Dan's Christmas

NOW one time it comes on Christmas, and in fact it is the evening before Christmas, and I am in Good Time Charley Bernstein's little speakeasy in West Forty-Seventh Street, wishing Charley a Merry Christmas and having a few hot Tom and Jerrys with him.

This hot Tom and Jerry is an old time drink that is once used by one and all in this country to celebrate Christmas with, and in fact it is once so popular that many people think Christmas is invented only to furnish an excuse for hot Tom and Jerry, although of course this is by no means true.

But anybody will tell you that there is nothing that brings out the true holiday spirit like hot Tom and Jerry, and I hear that since Tom and Jerry goes out of style in the United States, the holiday spirit is never quite the same.

The reason hot Tom and Jerry goes out of style is because it is necessary to use rum and one thing and another in making Tom and Jerry, and naturally when rum becomes illegal in this country Tom and Jerry is also against the law, because rum is something that is very hard to get around town these days.

For a while some people try making Tom and Jerry without putting rum in it, but somehow it never has the same old holiday spirit, so nearly everybody finally gives up in disgust, and this is not suprising, as making Tom and Jerry is by no means child's play. In fact, it takes quite an expert to make good

Tom and Jerry, and in the days when it is not illegal a good hot Tom and Jerry maker commands good wages and many friends.

Now of course Good Time Charley and I are not using rum in the Tom and Jerry we are making, as we do not wish to do anything illegal. What we are using is rye whisky that Good Time Charley gets on a doctor's prescription from a drug store, as we are personally drinking this hot Tom and Jerry and naturally we are not foolish enough to use any of Good Time Charley's own rye in it.

The prescription for the rye whisky comes from old Doc Moggs, who prescribes it for Good Time Charley's rheumatism in case Charley happens to get rheumatism, as Doc Moggs says there is nothing better for rheumatism than rye whisky, especially if it is made up in a hot Tom and Jerry. In fact, old Doc Moggs comes around and has a few seidels of hot Tom and Jerry with us for his own rheumatism.

He comes around during the afternoon, for Good Time Charley and I start making this Tom and Jerry early in the day, so as to be sure to have enough to last us over Christmas, and it is now along towards six o'clock, and our holiday spirit is practically one hundred per cent.

Well, as Good Time Charley and I are expressing our holiday sentiments to each other over our hot Tom and Jerry, and I am trying to think up the poem about the night before Christmas and all through the house, which I know will interest Charley no little, all of a sudden there is a big knock at the front door, and when Charley opens the door, who comes in carrying a large package under one arm but a guy by the name of Dancing Dan.

This Dancing Dan is a good-looking young guy, who always seems well-dressed, and he is called by the name of Dancing Dan because he is a great hand for dancing around and about with dolls in night clubs, and other spots where there is any dancing. In fact, Dan never seems to be doing anything else, although I hear rumors that when he is not dancing he is carrying on in a most illegal manner at one thing and another. But of course you can always hear rumors in this town about anybody, and personally I am rather fond of Dancing Dan as he always seems to be getting a great belt out of life.

Anybody in town will tell you that Dancing Dan is a guy with no Barnaby whatever in him, and in fact he has about as much gizzard as anybody around, although I wish to say I always question his judgment in dancing so much with Miss Muriel O'Neill, who works in the Half Moon night club. And the reason I question his judgment in this respect is because everybody knows that Miss Muriel O'Neill is a doll who is very well thought of by Heine Schmitz, and Heine Schmitz is not such a guy as will take kindly to anybody dancing more than once and a half with a doll that he thinks well of.

This Heine Schmitz is a very influential citizen of Harlem, where he has large interests in beer, and other business enterprises, and it is by no means violating any confidence to tell you that Heine Schmitz will just as soon blow your brains out as look at you. In fact, I hear sooner. Anyway, he is not a guy to monkey with and many citizens take the trouble to advise Dancing Dan that he is not only away out of line in dancing with Miss Muriel O'Neill, but that he is knocking his own price down to where he is no price at all.

But Dancing Dan only laughs ha-ha, and goes on dancing with Miss Muriel O'Neill anytime he gets the chance, and Good Time Charley says he does not blame him, at that, as Miss Muriel O'Neill is so beautiful that he will be dancing with her himself no matter what, if he is five years younger and can get a Roscoe out as fast as in the days when he runs with Paddy the Link and other fast guys.

Well, anyway, as Dancing Dan comes in, he weighs up the joint in one quick peek, and then he tosses the package he is carrying into a corner where it goes plunk, as if there is something very heavy in it, and then he steps up to the bar alongside of Charley and me and wishes to know what we are drinking.

RUNYON

Naturally we start boosting hot Tom and Jerry to Dancing Dan, and he says he will take a crack at it with us, and after
one crack, Dancing Dan says he will have another crack, and
Merry Christmas to us with it, and the first thing anybody knows
it is a couple of hours later and we still are still having cracks at
the hot Tom and Jerry with Dancing Dan, and Dan says he never
drinks anything so soothing in his life. In fact, Dancing Dan says
he will recommend Tom and Jerry to everybody he knows, only
he does not know anybody good enough for Tom and Jerry, except maybe Miss Muriel O'Neill, and she does not drink
anything with drugstore rye in it.

Well, several times while we are drinking this Tom and
Jerry, customers come to the door of Good Time Charley's little
speakeasy and knock, but by now Charley is commencing to be
afraid they will wish Tom and Jerry, too, and he does not feel we
will have enough for ourselves, so he hangs out a sign which
says "Closed on Account of Christmas," and the only one he will
let in is a guy by the name of Ooky, who is nothing but an old
rumdum, and who is going around all week dressed like Santa
Claus and carrying a sign advertising Moe Lewinsky's clothing
joint around in Sixth Avenue.

This Ooky is still wearing his Santa Claus outfit when
Charley lets him in, and the reason Charley permits such a character as Ooky in his joint is because Ooky does the porter work
for Charley when he is not Santa Claus for Moe Lewinsky, such
as sweeping out, and washing the glasses, and one thing and
another.

Well, it is about nine-thirty when Ooky comes in, and his
puppies are aching, and he is all petered out generally from
walking up and down and here and there with his sign, for any
time a guy is Santa Claus for Moe Lewinsky he must earn his
dough. In fact, Ooky is so fatigued, and his puppies hurt him so
much that Dancing Dan and Good Time Charley and I all feel
very sorry for him, and invite him to have a few mugs of hot
Tom and Jerry with us, and wish him plenty of Merry Christmas.

22

But old Ooky is not accustomed to Tom and Jerry and after about the fifth mug he folds up in a chair, and goes right to sleep on us. He is wearing a pretty good Santa Claus make-up, what with a nice red suit trimmed with white cotton, and a wig, and false nose, and long white whiskers, and a big sack stuffed with excelsior on his back, and if I do not know Santa Claus is not apt to be such a guy as will snore loud enough to rattle the windows, I will think Ooky is Santa Claus sure enough.

Well, we forget Ooky and let him sleep, and go on with our hot Tom and Jerry, and in the meantime we try to think up a few songs appropriate to Christmas, and Dancing Dan finally renders My Dad's Dinner Pail in a nice baritone and very loud, while I do first rate with Will You Love Me in December--As You Do in May? But personally I always think Good Time Charley Bernstein is a little out of line trying to sing a hymn in Jewish on such an occasion, and it causes words between us.

While we are singing many customers come tothe door and knock, and then read Charley's sign, and this seems to cause some unrest among them, and some of them stand outside saying it is a great outrage, until Charley sticks his noggin out the door and threatens to bust somebody's beezer if they do not go about their business and stop disturbing peaceful citizens.

Naturally the customes go away, as they do not wish their beezers busted, and Dancing Dan and Charley and I continue drinking along about bout midnight Dancing Dan wishes to see how he looks as Santa Claus.

So Good Time Charley and I help Dancing Dan pull off Ooky's outfit and put it on Dan, and this is easy as Ooky only has this Santa Claus outfit on over his ordinary clothes, and he does not even wake up when we are undressing him of the Santa Claus uniform.

Well, I wish to say I see many a Santa Claus in my time, but I never see a better looking Santa Claus than Dancing Dan, especially after he gets the wig and white whiskers fixed just right, and we put a sofa pillow that Good Time Charley happens to have around the joint for the cat to sleep on down his pants to give Dancing Dan a nice fat stomach such as Santa Claus is bound to have.

"Well," Charley finally says, "it is a great pity we do not know where there are some stockings hung up somewhere, because then," he says, "you can go around and stuff things in these stockings, as I always hear this is the main idea of a Santa Claus. But," Charley says, "I do not suppose anybody in this section has any stockings hung up, or if they have," he says, "the chances are they are so full of holes they will not hold anything. Anyway," Charley says, "even if there are any stockings hung up we do not have anything to stuff in them, although personally, " he says, "I will gladly donate a few pints of Scotch."

Well, I am pointing out that we have no reindeer and that a Santa Claus is bound to look like a terrible sap if he goes around without any reindeer, but Charley's remarks seem to give Dancing Dan an idea, for all of a sudden he speaks as follows:

"Why," Dancing Dan says, "I know where a stocking is hung up. It is hung up at Miss Muriel O'Neill's flat over here in West Forty-Ninth Street. This stocking is hung up by nobody but a party by the name of Gammer O'Neill, who is Miss Muriel O'Neill's grandmamma," Dancing Dan says. "Gammer O'Neill is going on ninety-odd," he says, "and Miss Muriel O'Neill told me she cannot hold out much longer, what with one thing and another, including being a little childish in spots.

"Now," Dancing Dan says, "I remember Miss Muriel O'Neill is telling me just the other night how Gammer O'Neill hangs up her stocking on Christmas Eve all her life, and," he says, "I judge from what Miss Muriel O'Neill says that the old doll always believes Santa Claus will come along one Christmas and fill the stocking full of beautiful gifts. But," Dancing Dan says, "Miss Muriel O'Neill tells me Santa Claus never does this, though Miss Muriel O'Neill personally always takes a few gifts home and puts them into the stocking to make Gammer O'Neill feel better.

"But, of course," Dancing Dan says, "these gifts are nothing much because Miss Muriel O'Neill is very poor, and proud, and also good, and will not take a dime off of anybody and I can lick the guy who says she will.

"Now," Dancing Dan goes on, "it seems that while Gammer O'Neill is very happy to get whatever she finds in her stocking on Christmas morning, she does not understand why Santa Claus is not more liberal, and," he says, "Miss Muriel O'Neill is saying to me that she only wishes she can give Gammer O'Neill one real big Christmas before the old doll puts her checks back in the rack.

"So," Dancing Dan states, "here is a job for us. Miss Muriel O'Neill and her grandmamma live all alone in this flat over in West Forty-ninth street, and," he says, "at such an hour as this Miss Muriel O'Neill is bound to be working, and the chances are Gammer O'Neill is sound asleep, and we will just hop over there and Santa Claus will fill up her stocking with beautiful gifts.

"Well, I say, I do not see where we are going to get any beautiful gifts at his time of night, what with all the stores being closed, unless we dash into an all-night drug store and buy a few bottles of perfume and a bum toilet set is guys always do when they forget about their ever-loving wives until after store hours on Christmas Eve, but Dancing Dan says never mind about this, but let us have a few more Tom and Jerrys first.

So we have a few more Tom and Jerrys and then Dancing Dan picks up he package he heaves into the corner, and dumps most of the excelsior out of Ooky's Santa Claus sack, and puts the bundle in, and Good Time Charley turns out all the lights, but one, and leaves a bottle of Scotch on the able in front of Ooky for a Christmas gift, and away we go.

Personally, I regret very much leaving the hot Tom and Jerry, but then I'm also very enthusiastic about going along to help Dancing Dan play Santa Claus, while Good Time Charley is practically overjoyed, as it is the first time in his life Charley is ever mixed up in so much holiday spirit.

As we go up Broadway, headed for Forty-ninth Street, Charley and I see many citizens we know and give them a large hello, and wish them Merry Christmas, and some of these citizens shake hands with Santa Claus, not knowing he is nobody but Dancing Dan, although later I understand there's some gossip among these citizens because they claim a Santa Claus with such a breath on him as our Santa Claus has is a little out of line.

And once we are somewhat embarrassed when a lot of little kids going home with their parents from a late Christmas party somewhere gather about Santa Claus with shouts of childish glee, and some of them wish to climb up Santa Claus' legs. Naturally, Santa Claus gets a little peevish, and calls them a few names, and one of the parents comes up and wishes to know what is the idea of Santa Claus using such language, and Santa Claus takes a punch at the parent, all of which is no doubt astonishing to the little kids who have an idea of Santa Claus as a very kindly old guy.

Well, finally we arrive in front of the place where Dancing Dan says Miss Muriel O'Neill and her grandmamma live, and it is nothing but a tenement house not far back off Madison Square Garden, and furthermore it is a walk-up, and at this time there are no lights burning in the joint except a gas jet in the main hall, and by the light of this jet we look at the names on the letter boxes, such as you always find in the hall of these joints, and we see that Miss Muriel O'Neill and her grandmamma live on the fifth floor.

This is the top floor, and personally I do not like the idea of walking up five flights of stairs, and I am willing to let Dancing Dan and Good Time Charley go, but Dancing Dan insists we must all go, and finally I agree with him because Charley is commencing to argue that the right way for us to do is to get on the roof and let Santa Claus go down a chimney, and is making so much noise I am afraid he will wake somebody up.

So up the stairs we climb and finally we come to a door on the top floor that has a little card in a slot that says O'Neill, so we know we reach our destination. Dancing Dan first tries the knob, and right away the door opens, and we are in a little two- or three-room flat, with not much furniture in it, and what furniture there is, is very poor. One single gas jet is burning near a bed in a room just off the one the door opens into, and by this light we see a very old doll is sleeping on the bed, so we judge this is nobody but Gammer O'Neill.

On her face is a large smile, as if she is dreaming of something very pleasant. On a chair at the head of the bed is hung a long black stocking, and it seems to be such a stocking as is often patched and mended, so I can see that what Miss Muriel O'Neill tells Dancing Dan about her grandmamma hanging up her stocking is really true, although up to this time I have my doubts. Finally Dancing Dan unslings the sack on his back, and takes out his package, and unties this package, and all of a sudden out pops a raft of big diamond bracelets, and diamond rings, and diamond brooches, and diamond necklaces, and I do not know what else in the way of diamonds, and Dancing Dan and I begin stuffing these diamonds into the stocking and Good Time Charley pitches in and helps us. There are enough diamonds to fill the stocking to the muzzle, and it is no small stocking, at that, and I judge that Gammer O'Neill has a pretty fair set of bunting sticks when she is young. In fact, there are so many diamonds that we have enough left over to make a nice little pile on the chair after we fill the stocking plumb up, leaving a nice diamond-studded vanity case sticking out the top where we figure it will hit Gammer O'Neill's eye when she wakes up. And it is not until I get out in the fresh air again that all of a sudden I remember seeing large headlines in the afternoon papers about a five hundred-G's stickup in the afternoon of one of the biggest diamond merchants in Maiden Lane while he is sitting in his office, and I also recall once hearing rumors that Dancing Dan is one of the best lone-hand git-'em-up guys in the world. Naturally, I commence to wonder if I am in the proper company when I am with Dancing Dan, even if he is Santa Claus. So I leave him on the next corner arguing with Good Time Charley about whether they ought to go and find some more presents somewhere, and look for other stockings to stuff, and I hasten on home and go to bed. The next day I find I have such a noggin that I do not care to stir around, and in fact I do not stir around much for a couple of weeks. Then one night I drop around to Good Time Charley's little speakeasy, and ask Charley what is doing.

"Well," Charley says, "many things are doing, and personally," he says, "I'm greatly surprised I do not see you at Gammer O'Neill's wake. You know Gammer O'Neill leaves this wicked old world a couple of days after Christmas," Good Time Charley says, "and," he says, "Miss Muriel O'Neill states that Doc Moggs claims it is at least a day after she is entitled to go, but she is sustained," Charley says, "by great happiness in finding her stocking filled with beautiful gifts on Christmas morning.

"According to Miss Muriel O'Neill," Charley says, "Gammer O'Neill dies practically convinced that there is a Santa Claus, although of course," he says, "Miss Muriel O'Neill does not tell her the real owner of the gifts, an all-right guy by the name of Shapiro leaves the gifts with her after Miss Muriel O'Neill notifies him of finding of same.

"It seems," Charley says, "this Shapiro is a tender-hearted guy, who is willing to help keep Gammer O'Neill with us a little longer when Doc Moggs says leaving the gifts with her will do it.

"So," Charley says, "everything is quite all right, as the coppers cannot figure anything except that maybe the rascal who takes the gifts from Shapiro gets conscience-stricken, and leaves them the first place he can, and Miss Muriel O'Neill receives a ten-G's reward for finding the gifts and returning them. "And," Charley says, "I hear Dancing Dan is in San Francisco and is figuring on reforming and becoming a dancing teacher, so he can marry Miss Muriel O'Neill, and of course," he says, "we all hope and trust she never learns any details of Dancing Dan's career."

Well, it is Christmas Eve a year later that I run into a guy by the name of Shotgun Sam, who is mobbed up with Heine Schmitz in Harlem, and who is a very, very obnoxious character indeed.

"Well, well, well," Shotgun says, "the last time I see you is another Christmas like this, and you are coming out of Good Time Charley's joint, and," he says, "you certainly have your pots on."

"Well, Shotgun," I says, "I am sorry you get such a wrong impression of me, but the truth is," I say, "on the occasion you speak of, I am suffering from a dizzy feeling in my head."

"It is all right with me," Shotgun says. "I have a tip this guy Dancing Dan is in Good Time Charley's the night I see you, and Mockie Morgan, and GunnerJack and me are casing the joint, because," he says, "Heine Schmitz is all sored up at Dan over some doll, although of course," Shotgun says, "it is all right now, as Heine has another doll.

"Anyway," he says, "we never get to see Dancing Dan. We watch the joint from six-thirty in the evening until daylight Christmas morning, and nobody goes in all night but old Ooky the Santa Claus guy in his Santa Claus makeup, and," Shotgun says, "nobody comes out except you and Good Time Charley and Ooky.

"Well," Shotgun says, "it is a great break for Dancing Dan he never goes in or comes out of Good Time Charley's, at that, because," he says, "we are waiting for him on the second-floor front of the building across the way with some nice little sawed-offs, and are under orders from Heine not to miss."

"Well, Shotgun," I say, "Merry Christmas."

"Well, all right," Shotgun says, "Merry Christmas."

The End

29

Death Pays a Social Call

DEATH came in and sat down beside me, a large and most distinguished-looking figure in beautifully-tailored soft, white flannels. His expansive face wore a big smile.

"Oh, hello," I said. "Hello, hello, hello. I was not expecting you. I have not looked at the red board lately and did not know my number was up. If you will just hand me my kady and my coat I will be with you in a jiffy."

"Tut-tut-tut," Death said. "Not so fast. I have not come for you. By no means."

"You haven't?" I said.

"No," Death said.

"Then what the hell are you doing here?" I demanded indignantly. "What do you mean by barging in here without even knocking and depositing your fat Francis in my easiest chair without so much as by-your-leave?"

"Excuse me," Death said, taken aback at my vehemence. "I was in your neighbourhood and all tired out after my day's work and I thought I would just drop in and sit around with you awhile and cut up old scores. It is merely a social call, but I guess I owe you an apology at that for my entrance.

"I should say you do," I said.

"Well, you see I am so accustomed to entering doors without knocking that I never thought," Death said. "If you like, I will go outside and knock and not come in until you answer."

"Look," I said. "You can get out of here and stay out of here. Screw, bum!"

Death burst out crying.

Huge tears rolled down both pudgy cheeks and splashed on his white silk lapels.

"There it is again," he sobbed. "That same inhospitable note wherever I go. No one wants to chat with me. I am so terribly lonesome. I thought surely you would like to punch the bag with me awhile."

I declined to soften up.

"Another thing," I said sternly, "what are you doing in that get-up? You are supposed to be in black. You are supposed to look sombre, not like a Miami Beach Winter tourist."

"Why," Death said, "I got tired of wearing my old working clothes all the time. Besides, I thought these garments would be more cheerful and informal for a social call."

"Well, beat it" I said. Just Duffy out of here."

"You need not fear me," Death said.

"I do not fear you Deathie, old boy," I said, "but you are a knock to me among my neighbours. Your visit is sure to get noised about and cause gossip. You know you are not considered a desirable character by many persons, although, mind you, I am not saying anything against you."

"Oh, go ahead," Death said. "Everybody else puts the zing on me so you might as well, too. But I did not think your neighbours would recognize me in white, although, come to think of it, I noticed everybody running to their front door and grabbing in their 'Welcome' mats as I went past. Why are you shivering if you do not fear me?"

"I am shivering because of that clammy chill you brought in with you," I said "You lug the atmosphere of a Frigidaire around with you."

"You don't tell me?" Death said. "I must correct that. I must pack an electric pad with me. Do you think that is why I seem so unpopular wherever I go? Do you think I will ever be a social success?"

"I am inclined to doubt it," I said. "Your personality repels many persons. I do not find it so bad as that of some others I know, but you have undoubtedly developed considerable sales resistance to yourself in various quarters."

"Do you think it would do any good if I hired a publicity man? Death asked. "I mean, to conduct a campaign to make me popular?"

"It might," I said. "The publicity men have worked wonders with even worse cases than your. But see here, D., I am not going to waste my time giving you advice and permitting you to linger on in my quarters to get me talked about. Kindly do a scrammola, will you?"

Death had halted his tears for a moment, but now he turned on all faucets, crying boo-hoo-hoo-hoo.

"I am so lonesome," he said between lachrymose heaves.

"Git!" I said.

"Everybody is against me," Death said.

He slowly exited and, as I heard his tears falling plop-plop-plop to the floor as he passed down the hallway, I thought of the remark of Agag, the king of the Amalekites, to Samuel just before Samuel mowed him down: "Surely the bitterness of death is past."

The End

Also from Benediction Books ...
Wandering Between Two Worlds: Essays on Faith and Art
Anita Mathias
Benediction Books, 2007
152 pages
ISBN: 0955373700

Available from www.amazon.com, www.amazon.co.uk

In these wide-ranging lyrical essays, Anita Mathias writes, in lush, lovely prose, of her naughty Catholic childhood in Jamshedpur, India; her large, eccentric family in Mangalore, a sea-coast town converted by the Portuguese in the sixteenth century; her rebellion and atheism as a teenager in her Himalayan boarding school, run by German missionary nuns, St. Mary's Convent, Nainital; and her abrupt religious conversion after which she entered Mother Teresa's convent in Calcutta as a novice. Later rich, elegant essays explore the dualities of her life as a writer, mother, and Christian in the United States-- Domesticity and Art, Writing and Prayer, and the experience of being "an alien and stranger" as an immigrant in America, sensing the need for roots.

About the Author

Anita Mathias was born in India, has a B.A. and M.A. in English from Somerville College, Oxford University and an M.A. in Creative Writing from the Ohio State University. Her essays have been published in The Washington Post, The London Magazine, The Virginia Quarterly Review, Commonweal, Notre Dame Magazine, America, The Christian Century, Religion Online, The Southwest Review, Contemporary Literary Criticism, New Letters, The Journal, and two of HarperSanFrancisco's The Best Spiritual Writing anthologies. Her non-fiction has won fellowships from The National Endowment for the Arts; The Minnesota State Arts Board; The Jerome Foundation, The Vermont Studio Center; The Virginia Centre for the Creative Arts, and the First Prize for the Best General Interest Article from the Catholic Press Association of the United States and Canada. Anita has taught Creative Writing at the College of William and Mary, and now lives and writes in Oxford, England.

www.anitamathias.com
wanderingbetweentwoworlds.blogspot.com (General and Culture)
thegoodbooksblog.blogspot.com (Reading and Writing)
theoxfordchristian.blogspot.com (Christian)